For Brian, Gabriel, and Sasha,
who fill my world with love
—G. S.

To Lin
—G. B.

SIMON & SCHUSTER BOOKS FOR YOUNG READERS
An imprint of Simon & Schuster Children's Publishing Division
1230 Avenue of the Americas, New York, New York 10020
Text copyright © 2007 by Gillian Shields
Illustrations copyright © 2007 by Gary Blythe
First published in Great Britain in 2007 by Simon & Schuster UK Ltd
First U.S. edition 2008
All rights reserved, including the right of reproduction in whole or in part in any form.
SIMON & SCHUSTER BOOKS FOR YOUNG READERS is a trademark of Simon & Schuster, Inc.
The text for this book is set in Garamond.
The illustrations for this book are rendered in oil paint.
Manufactured in China
2 4 6 8 10 9 7 5 3 1
CIP data for this book is available from the Library of Congress.
ISBN-13: 978-1-4169-5363-0
ISBN-10: 1-4169-5363-9

The Perfect Bear

GILLIAN SHIELDS & GARY BLYTHE

Simon & Schuster Books for Young Readers
New York London Toronto Sydney

There once was a girl who was a bit like you.
She was not too big. She was not too small. She was just
somewhere nicely in the middle.

One day a bear arrived from the store. He was very grand.
He had soft white fur, and a little red hat, and a magic key.
When the girl turned the key, the bear sang a song.
He was very proud of his finery.

The old pink rabbit, who sat on the chest of drawers, said,
"Hello! What's your name?"
The bear replied haughtily, "My name is Do Not Touch."
In the shop, there had been a sign next to him that read,
DO NOT TOUCH, and the bear thought it was a very good name.

But the girl didn't seem to understand.
She wanted to touch him, and hold him, and play with him!
The bear didn't like this one little bit.

The girl took the bear to the park, but he lost his hat.
She took the bear to the beach, but his fur
became full of sand.

She painted his picture but accidentally splashed him.

Once, she even left him out in the rain.

The bear was very angry that his white fur was getting dirty.

"Poor Bear!" said the girl one day. "You need a bath."
The Do Not Touch bear trembled with fear. The soap stung
his eyes. The clothespins pinched his ears. And when he was dry,
his beautiful soft white fur wasn't as white, or soft,
or beautiful as it had been before.

Then something dreadful happened.
When the girl turned his key, there was a
horrible squeaking noise. The bear couldn't sing!
The bathwater had ruined his music box.

"Oh, dear," said the girl, "I'll have to take it out."
She fetched her doctor's kit.
"Don't worry, Bear," she whispered. "It won't hurt."
"DO NOT TOUCH!" shouted the bear.
But the girl didn't seem to understand.

When she had finished, the girl held the bear in front of the mirror.
He saw a small, gray reflection with a hollow place in its center
sewn up with big black stitches.
The bear sighed. It didn't matter if people touched him now.
He wasn't a Do Not Touch bear anymore.
He was just any old bear.

But the girl said a strange thing.
"You're much more cuddly without your music box, Bear."
And she started to take him to bed with her, every night.

The bear liked the night,

when no one could see how shabby he had become.

Every night, the girl held him close and told him stories.

When she fell asleep, the bear would lie awake,

his brown eyes gleaming as if they had tears in them.

The old pink rabbit looked down and asked kindly,

"What's the matter, Bear?"

"I want all my finery back," cried the bear,

"so that everyone will admire me."

"It's so much better to be loved than admired, you know,"

said the old pink rabbit.

"What is love?" asked the bear.

"It's what we're all about, little silly," laughed

the old pink rabbit.

"Hats and fur and keys don't matter. They're only on the outside.

It's what's inside us that's important."

The bear started to wonder what was inside the girl.

He noticed that she dressed him warmly if it was cold.

She gave him honey to eat.

She sewed up the hole in his middle when it came apart.

And one night, the girl said softly, "I love you, Bear,"

before falling asleep. But the bear stayed awake all night long, thinking.

The next day, the girl went with her mother to
a big department store. They looked at shoes and suitcases
and saucepans, but when it was time to go home,
the girl said, "I've lost my Bear!"

The girl and her mother looked everywhere.
The bear wasn't near the shoes, or the suitcases, or the saucepans.
He wasn't anywhere. He was lost.
The girl tried not to cry.

In the Lost Property department, a small gray bear was feeling
very strange. He suddenly realized that he wanted to see the girl again,
more than anything in the world. He had the oddest
feeling in the empty place where his old music box had been.
It was . . . love.

Then the bear saw his girl running toward him.
She was not too big. She was not too small.
She was just somewhere perfect in the middle.

"I'm so sorry, Bear," said the girl. "I'll never, never
lose you again. Oh, I do love you!"
"I love you too! I love you too!" cried the bear,
trying to make her hear.
And this time, the girl really did understand.

If anyone asks the bear now what he is called, he says,
"My name is Bear. Just Bear."
And the place inside him that used to be empty
is now full of happiness.